Smuggler!

by

Martyn Beardsley

Illustrated by Dylan Gibson

First published in 2008 in Great Britain by
Barrington Stoke Ltd
18 Walker Street, Edinburgh, EH3 7LP

www.barringtonstoke.co.uk

ISBN: 978-1-84299-537-2

Printed in Great Britain by Bell & Bain Ltd

Contents

Before the Beginning ...   1

1 Times of Change   8

2 Heading Home   10

3 The New Order   16

4 The Look-out   22

5 Prisoner   31

6 The Chase   39

... After the End   54

Fabulous facts from ye Days of
Smuggling!   57

Author and Illustrator fact files   64

Before the Beginning ...

Jack was bored. His parents were getting all excited about the new house they were moving into. But the problem was, it wasn't new. It was old and falling down, and the work to put it right seemed to go on for ever. Why didn't they just pull it down and build a *proper* new house?

Jack already lived in a nice house just outside London, but his parents had made up their minds to move so that they could be near the sea. They had found this tumble-down old cottage near a village called Lyme Regis. And now the family had to spend all their spare time coming out here hammering, sawing, and getting sore and dirty.

A house builder called Dan was doing most of the important work, with Mum and Dad helping him out. Jack and his little sister Emily did the odd job here and there, and Jack was allowed to hammer some nails in now and then, but most of the time they sat around with nothing to do. It was boring, boring, boring. But things were about to change ...

Dad was hacking away at the wall next to the old fire-place. Suddenly, he stopped work. "What on earth's this?"

Mum came over and peered into a small hole in the side of the wall. "It looks like a secret compartment!"

Words like *secret compartment* were too promising to ignore, and in an instant Jack and Emily had run over to join the adults.

Everyone was peering into the dark hole, apart from Dan the builder. He was standing back, looking at the wall and chimney. "I thought there was something odd about it. This wall seems much thicker than the others – it's almost as if there's something behind the chimney and fire-place ..."

Just then, Mrs Gibbs from next door came in. She was a cheerful old lady who often popped round to bring them a cup of tea while they worked. Today, she had someone with her – an even older man, little and round with white hair and bushy white eyebrows. "This is George Mutter, an old friend of mine from Uplyme," Mrs Gibbs said.

"We've found a smuggler's hole!" Emily, Jack's sister, said. Emily was always saying things like that. She was always so childish.

But out of the blue, Mr Mutter, speaking in a voice that made him sound like a smuggler or a pirate himself, said, "She probably be right as well! Come and see!"

He shuffled outside on stiff little legs, and everyone followed apart from Dan the builder and Jack's dad, who were so eager to see what was behind the fire-place that they carried on bashing at the bricks.

Outside in the sunshine, Mr Mutter stood half-way down the garden path looking back at the cottage. "There y'are!" he said. He was pointing his crooked, bony finger at what looked like two circles of dark glass set into the cracked and crumbling plaster on the wall, just below the roof. They looked to Jack like the bottoms of two green bottles. And as a matter of fact, they were!

"That used to be a secret sign!" said Mr Mutter. "When smugglers were bringing their goods from the beach, they knew they could safely bring them to a house where they saw that sign."

Just then, there were shouts of surprise from inside the cottage, and everyone rushed in to see what Dan and Jack's father had found.

Hidden between the back of the chimney and the outside wall of the house was a narrow space. On the floor were two wooden barrels and some, dusty, cobweb-covered bottles and boxes.

"Smugglers' treasure!" said Jack. Emily had been right!

"But why would they leave it all here? None of it has been touched!" his mum said.

Jack's dad was grinning. "This might tell us!" He waved a letter. It was written in small, spidery writing on yellowing paper. They opened it up with great excitement and began to read ...

Chapter 1
Times of Change

My Dear Cousin Jem,

You will be pleased to find with this letter the goods from France. Your mother informed me that you are at this time out in your boat fishing off Start Point, and it was she who gave me the key to your home so that I could leave the goods here. My father believes a big storm is heading this way, and

I do hope you are back safe and dry before the waves grow too high.

But I must include in these lines another warning. For I beg to inform you that great changes appear to be taking place in the Free Trade upon which so many of us have come to rely. We learned this to our great alarm on our return to Lyme after three weeks away. It seems we must now all have our wits about us more than ever before.

I will now tell you what troubles my father and myself have suffered these past few days. I write it as a warning to you, and a sign of what we might now all expect ...

Chapter 2
Heading Home

So Jem, we set sail from France with a light breeze at our backs and with happy hearts. We had done good business, and were returning with barrels of brandy and rum, together with some tea and French lace of the highest quality.

Poor people such as ourselves cannot afford to buy this stuff at the normal price because of the high taxes. Yet by bringing

them here in secret and paying no taxes, we can sell them at a price people can buy at.

Times have been hard on the likes of us since the war against Napoleon, as you know only too well, cousin Jem. The little money we, and many others like us in Lyme, make in this way can mean the difference between having a proper meal or going to bed with our stomachs empty. Who could blame us? Apart from, that is, the Revenue Men who try to catch us!

Yet the risks are great in our line of work, Jem. The Revenue Service has look-outs and Riding Officers along the cliffs. And then there is their ship, called *Falcon*, a Revenue cutter that prowls the waters off Lyme looking out for boats such as ours. At least we have the comfort of knowing that old Captain Ellis of the *Falcon*, is from Lyme himself. He understands what life is like for folks like us and why we do what we do. Very often, when he does manage to catch us, if two barrels of brandy happen to break free and roll his way his search of our boat is not a very careful one!

But Jem, I have told you that changes are afoot.

At first, all seemed well. We made good time on our crossing. The rays of the rising sun lit up the cliffs of Golden Cap. This landmark was a welcome sight to us as our home port came into view. Samuel Hobson, our look-out, shouted that he had spotted a large sail off our starboard bow. No one took too much notice, as Lyme is a busy port. But soon he called again: "She be a Revenue cutter!"

"Haul to," ordered my father. "Let us hang back a while and give her time to clear the bay." He turned to me. "Edward – go below and bring up a little wine in case Captain

Ellis is feeling bored today and sends the *Falcon* after us!"

But the lookout shook his head. "It's not the *Falcon*, Jack."

"But you said she was the Revenue cutter, man!"

"I said she be *a* Revenue cutter. This one is different. Bigger, newer, faster."

Work on board our little ship stopped, and all eyes turned to the strange sail coming out of Lyme Bay. So far, it was just a small speck in the distance, but another of our men grabbed a telescope and went to the side for a better view. "She's changed course!" he cried. "She's headed right for us – *and she's putting up the red flag!*"

My heart sank. The long red flag, in the shape of a triangle, at the mast-head was a signal that she was giving chase. "Turn about,

father!" I begged him. "We can head for Cornwall. She'll never follow us all that way."

My father was silent for what seemed like an age, gazing at the ship. "She would follow us to the ends of the earth," he said. "Prepare to be boarded."

Although it was not the order they expected, the crew obeyed right away. Forgive me if I seem too full of pride in my father, Jem. But we have all sailed with him long enough to know to trust Jack Ford.

Chapter 3
The New Order

"I am Lieutenant Charles Richardson, of His Majesty's Revenue cutter, *Dart*. I have come on board to carry out a search for smuggled goods."

I must admit, Jem, that I was somewhat impressed by the tall young officer who had rowed across with six stout men – each of them armed with a musket and a cutlass. He was wearing a splendid naval uniform of dark blue with gold buttons and trimmings. There was a confident air about him for one so young, though perhaps he had too serious and stern a manner.

"And what makes you think we might have smuggled goods on our little boat?" asked my father lightly, as if completely puzzled that a Revenue man should take an interest in him.

"I know that many smugglers operate in these waters," said the young officer, "and I have heard of you, Jack Ford."

"Then you will know that I am just a poor fisherman!"

"Where, then, are the fish you have caught?"

My father smiled and gave a shrug. "It's been a very bad trip."

Some of our men were grinning – but the Revenue man wasn't. "Oh, I suspect you have had a very good trip, Jack Ford. But not catching fish. Men, search this boat from top to bottom!"

While his men sprang into action, my father leaned against the mast and lit his pipe as if he hadn't a care in the world. Yet every nook and cranny of our vessel was inspected, and the searchers clearly knew all the smuggler's tricks for hiding his goods. There wasn't a chance of them missing anything.

After a full hour, Lieutenant Richardson's second-in-command returned to make his report.

"Er ... nothing found, sir."

Lieutenant Richardson's face was a picture. "Nothing?"

"Not a thing, sir." He looked like an old hand himself and would have known the ways of the Free Traders. He must have known that we had hidden our goods in a much safer place than the bottom of the boat. We had hidden them in the sea! The barrels had been tied together with weights on them to make them sink. There was one empty barrel tied on the end which would float on the surface to help us find our treasure when we came back to collect it later. My father calls this method of fooling the Revenue men, "sowing the crop"!

Lieutenant Richardson was most put out, Jem. But we still had to come back in the night to collect our barrels – and far from having solved our problems, we were soon to find that we had even greater challenges to face.

Chapter 4
The Look-out

When we got to shore my father visited the Royal Standard Inn for some food and drink. There he learned of the changes which had taken place while we were away. It seems that with the war against Napoleon now over, the Navy has taken charge of the Revenue cutters. Many of the old men like Captain Ellis have lost their jobs. Naval officers, fresh from battles at sea with the French, have taken their place and are keen to do just as good a job for the Revenue Service.

We waited for darkness to fall. I went up onto Black Ven Cliff with my father's telescope to try to spot our marker barrel and keep watch on the *Dart* Revenue cutter – but she was at anchor and stayed there the rest of the day. There was a reason for this, as we were to discover to our cost. My father had got together some trusted local men to meet him with carts in Charton Bay at dusk. All was set for us to reclaim from the sea that which we believed was rightly ours.

We met up in the bay as the sun began to sink into the western sea, and it felt suddenly much colder. A stiff wind whipped the white froth from the waves and I felt the icy sea spray sting my cheeks. Before long, we saw two boats being rowed round Humble Point. In one was my father, and in the other his old friend Tom Sherwin, landlord of the Royal Standard Inn. Once the boats were as close to shore as they could come, the men waded out through the freezing water and clambered into them. Everyone knew his job, and not a word was spoken.

The only person to stay behind, sadly, was me. Being still a child, they didn't think I was strong enough to pull on oars or handle heavy barrels (but I hope that at least you, Jem, know that I can do both). My duty was just as important, however, as I was the look-out. Once the boats had pulled silently away, with sacking tied around the oars to help muffle any sound, I scrambled up the cliff to take up my post.

It was a clear but chilly night. Even with the sun now gone, I found it still light enough to watch the boats head out into the choppy sea. This made my task easier, but I was still worried – for I knew it would also be easier for anyone else who might be watching that night ...

It took the two boats a long time to make their way towards the spot where the barrels had been sunk. They became nothing but black specks, like insects crawling across the floor. Every now and then the little boats were lost from view when they rose and fell in the rolling seas as they slowly but surely reached the marker barrel.

It was then that I spotted another black speck. Only one, but it seemed as big as our two. It looked as if it was coming from the direction of Lyme. I quickly put the telescope to my eye. All I could see was that it was a large rowing boat – such as those used by the Revenue Service.

With my heart suddenly pounding, I snatched up my fire making things, and struck the flint again and again on the steel until a spark set light to the tinder. I then carefully placed it among the pile of twigs and branches I had made ready. This was the first time in my life I had ever had to light a warning fire to the men out at sea, and my hands were shaking.

At first, the fire stuttered and almost died. I blew hard into the bottom of the pile the way I had seen the older men do, and soon, thankfully, it blazed into life. I felt that God must be watching over me, helping me to protect my father and the others, and said a little prayer of thanks under my breath.

Now I grabbed my telescope again. But even in such a short space of time the night had grown darker. And after gazing into the fire, I found I could no longer see into the darkness nearly so well. I could make out neither our boats nor those of the Revenue men. I found myself having to do two things at once – searching the moonlit sea with the telescope, and making sure the fire kept blazing so it could be seen from far away. I had no idea whether our boats had seen the warning signal, or even whether they had already been taken by the Revenue men.

I cursed Lieutenant Richardson, as I was sure he would be in command of the boat sneaking through the waves to try and catch our men. But I was wrong.

A firm hand grabbed my arm, making me jump and cry out with fright. I twisted round despite the powerful grip I was in – and Jem, I saw none other than Lieutenant Richardson glaring down at me!

"Child, lighting a warning fire is just as much a crime as smuggling itself," he said darkly. "I arrest you in the name of the King. Come with me."

And with that, he dragged me, struggling and shouting, down the hillside and into Lyme.

Chapter 5
Prisoner

In the short time that my father has considered me old enough to help him in his Free Trade work, I have been in a few scrapes and close shaves. I think myself at least a little braver than many boys of my age. But that night, I felt fear that I would never have believed possible. I must admit that as I was dragged through the streets of Lyme I cried and screamed like a tiny tot who believes the Bogey Man is after him.

Everyone stopped to look at the carry-on, and some laughed. But I didn't care, because I knew what was waiting for me. Many parents warn their little ones that the Bogey Man will get them if they are naughty. But you know as well as I, Jem, that parents of children from Lyme also use another threat. That they will be sent to the *Lock-Up*. It had always seemed just as much a fairy tale to me as the Bogey Man – but that was where I was to go.

As he marched me down Bridge Street towards that awful place, the sight of the heavy wooden door with its black iron studs seemed even more terrifying than normal in the evening gloom. Once we were outside the Lock-Up – that grim, stone building on the corner of the Town Hall – Lieutenant Richardson gripped my collar tightly with one hand and took out a jangling bunch of enormous keys from his pocket with the other.

I'm glad you couldn't see me then, Jem – the whole town must have heard my screams. He picked out the largest of the keys and unlocked the door. It creaked open to show a black hole which to me seemed like the entrance to hell itself. He pushed me inside, saying, "I'd give you a candle, but there's straw on the floor and you'd probably end up setting fire to the place."

With that, the door slammed shut, and I was left alone. The room was in almost complete darkness. A little feeble light came from a small window set too high up for anyone to see through its iron bars. The smells in that place were so awful that although I could feel the straw beneath my feet, I hardly dared sit or lie down on it. (It wasn't till morning that I discovered a wooden bed against one wall.)

In the end, I kicked away the straw from one of the corners of the Lock-Up and slumped down with my back against the wall, weeping bitterly at my bad luck. I heard people walking past outside now and then. Once I heard voices I knew, and shrank further down, as if they might be able to see me in my shameful state.

I soon lost all sense of time. Ten minutes seemed like ten hours – and worse still I had no idea how long I was to remain a prisoner

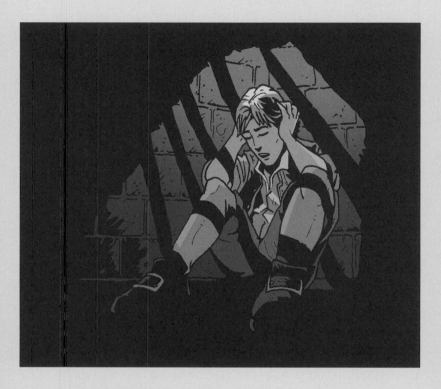

in that hellish place. Might it be days?
Weeks? An image of my mother hearing
about where I was and sobbing through the
night flashed into my mind, and my heart
felt heavy with shame. I should have been too
clever and alert to allow myself to be caught
by any Revenue officer. I suspected some of
the men thought I was too young to do a
man's job – and now they had been proved

right. I could picture them, safe and warm in their homes at this very moment, laughing about what a fool I was. My eyes stung with fresh tears.

That night seemed to last forever, and I was sure I would get no sleep at all. Yet I must have dozed off at some point, for the next thing I knew I was woken from a nightmare by the sound of the key in the door. As I struggled to my senses and rubbed the sleep from my still moist eyes, the grey light of morning came through the opening door, and a ghost-like figure was framed within it.

"Is that you, son?"

I jumped to my feet and ran towards him. *"Father!"*

My tears came again as we hugged, but this time they were tears of happiness and relief. Then I heard the voice of Lieutenant Richardson behind my father.

"You may go now, boy. But you shall stand trial in court at the next Assizes – don't forget that."

My joy was crushed by the thought of being found guilty and of spending many more nights like the last, but this time in Exeter Jail. Many local smugglers had been sent there – and by all accounts it was far, far worse than the Lock-Up.

Chapter 6
The Chase

My father took me home and gave me breakfast, and after I had been greeted by my sisters and mother, and answered all their questions about my ordeal, he told me what had happened after I had been arrested.

Our men had seen my signal! In their eyes, it seems, I was something of a hero. They had not noticed the Revenue ship heading towards them, and my cliff top fire had saved them all from suffering the same fate as me. They turned their boats about, slipped away from the Revenue men, put in at a little bay along the coast and made their way home.

The biggest surprise was when my father told me that he was going again to try and get the goods we had thrown overboard. He was going to do it that morning, in broad daylight!

"If it's left too long, it might spoil and become useless to us. I can't afford that." He finished his last slice of bread and got to his feet.

"Then I shall come with you!" I cried, pushing my chair back and standing up.

My mother cried out, and my father said, "You have done more than enough already, son. Stay here with your mother."

But I wouldn't be put off. "I will be with you this time. If they take us, we shall be together. Whatever happens, I will stand by your side, father!"

He looked at my mother, and we could both tell from her face what she thought on the matter. But he clapped me on the back. "You're a good lad. Come, we've got work to do."

But the morning did not go as I thought it would. My father and I, and some of our other regular men, hung about the Cobb for around three hours, mending fishing nets and doing other little jobs. Whenever I asked him when we were going, he would only reply, "When the time is right."

Just before midday, I heard a pistol shot coming from somewhere up on the cliffs, followed by a second a minute later. This, it turned out, was a signal from the Revenue look-out that a suspicious sail had been spotted. Within minutes, Lieutenant Richardson and his crew had set their sails, raised the anchor, and were making their way out to sea in the *Dart*.

"Now is our chance, lads!" said my father. We all scrambled onto our own boat, the *Mayfly*, and were soon sailing out while the speedy *Dart* went off in chase of some other poor boat.

It didn't take us long to find the spot where we had dropped our barrels overboard. And just a few minutes later our look-out had caught sight of the empty marker barrel, floating on the surface and tied by a rope to the rest of our goods. We pulled everything up on board and headed back to Lyme.

However, our run of bad luck was not yet over. We had been so busy loading the barrels that we had not seen the return of the *Dart*. I can only think that the ship she had chased down had no smuggled goods on it, and Lieutenant Richardson had ordered an immediate return to port.

This time, my father didn't need to stop and think what to do. "We have the wind at our backs, lads," he called to our crew. "Let's see just how fast this Revenue cutter is – we shall make a run for it!"

The crew gave a loud cheer, and we crowded on all sail and made for Seaton, the closest port to Lyme in a direction which would take us away from the *Dart*.

Our lookout soon shouted that the *Dart* had put up her red flag. This meant that she was coming after us, which came as no surprise. We knew she was a much faster sailer than us, and could only hope that our head-start would allow us to beat her into Seaton – where we had many friends – and hide our goods. If Lieutenant Richardson didn't catch us with the smuggled items, he could not arrest us.

I ran back to the stern of the ship and caught my first glimpse of the *Dart*. Its enormous main-sail was straining in the wind as she chased us.

"Lord, she *is* fast," said Samuel Hobson, one of our men. "This will be a close-run thing."

Just then, I noticed a puff of grey smoke billow from our distant enemy. Samuel Hobson dived to the deck and pulled me down

with him. "She's firing on us!" A second later, we heard a great splash in the water quite some way away from us.

"She'll never stop us with aiming like that!" I said trying to sound cheerful and brave, despite the fear I was feeling inside. I had never been under fire from another ship before.

Samuel Hobson's reply did nothing to help my nerves. "That was a warning shot and not meant to hit us," he said. "The *Dart* has Navy gunners on board now, men who have fought the French. There are none better in the world, and the next shot will be aimed at us if we don't take down our sails."

Almost as soon as he had finished speaking, I heard a horrible shriek high above us, quickly followed by a violent ripping sound. I looked up and saw that one of our smaller sails had been torn open by a cannon ball, leaving it flapping in the wind like washing on a line.

Before I could quite take this in, there was a huge crash, and great splinters of wood as long and as sharp as swords hissed viciously through the air in all directions. The third shot had completely smashed the wooden stairway leading down below. We were lucky – no one seemed to have been hurt.

"She's got our range," cried William Bowles. "Two more hits, and we shall be crippled if not sunk!"

My father was watching the *Dart* carefully through his telescope. "She will have to change tack any moment and won't be able to fire at us until she has finished making her turn. We press on!"

This raised another cheer from our men – which was cut short when one cannon ball flashed over our heads and landed in the sea ahead, sending up a great plume of water.

Seconds later, we heard a sickening crunch, and felt our whole boat shudder so violently that several men fell over. We had been hit between wind and water, Jem! There was a jagged hole in the side of the boat.

"The cutter's starting to tack," yelled our lookout. But there were no cheers this time. We were within sight of Seaton now – close enough to make out people on the shore, but the water rushing in was bound to slow us down even if it didn't sink us. As soon as the cutter had finished making her turn she would be after us again, and catching us even faster than before.

There was now a worried shout from one of the look-outs with a telescope: "She's preparing to lower the boats!" With our ship crippled, they would be able to send a couple of boat-loads across, full of men armed with guns and swords to arrest us. The memories of the Lock-Up came flooding back into my mind, making me shiver, and almost believe I would rather throw myself overboard into the icy water than go back to that place.

But then my father shouted to two of our men, "Take that damaged sail down. Use it to

plug the hole down below as best you can."
This they did, and sent word that they were
keeping the leak down to a trickle.

I kept my eyes fixed firmly on the *Dart*,
and she was by now so close that I could
make out two of her crew working in the
rigging. But she was no longer firing –
perhaps because we were so close to Seaton
that a stray cannon ball might have gone

into the port itself, where there were many boats at anchor.

To my surprise and joy, we began to surge forward once more. The quick-thinking repairs meant that we were soon back at almost full speed again. The *Dart* was delayed by having to lift her boats back up, yet soon she was gaining on us once more. But how clumsy those Seaton fishing boats are, Jem! So many of them seemed to get in the Revenue ship's way (by mistake, of course!) that she could not seem to get a good run at us.

Well, Jem, as you will know from the safe delivery of your goods, *we made it!* We got into Seaton just ahead of the Revenue ship, and helping hands waiting there made sure our smuggled goods "vanished" before the *Dart* could come along-side us. Richardson soon caught us – but yet again we were empty-handed!

And before coming here, I heard more good news about my upcoming trial in court, about which I was so worried. The judge is to be Sir John Graham. As you know, in secret he puts up the money for half of the Free Trade operations in our little part of the world, and there is yet to be one man found guilty of smuggling in one of his courts!

And so, Cousin Jem, beware the new Revenue men – but when you open the brandy which has arrived here safely despite all these dangers and adventures, drink a toast to me and the gallant crew of the little *Mayfly!*

Your dear Cousin,

Edward Ford

This day, the 26th April, 1816.

... After the End

Jack's dad put down the letter, and everyone remained silent for a moment as they tried to take it all in. Despite learning that the young smuggler Edward Ford and his father had escaped, Jack felt sad. He thought back to the part at the beginning of the letter about Jem being out fishing when a big storm was coming. The fact that the barrels were still here, and like the letter, had not been opened, must have meant that poor Jem had been lost at sea.

Then old Mr Mutter said something to
Mrs Gibbs, who went away for a while and
came back with a bottle of lemonade and
some glasses. Mr Mutter cleared away the
cobwebs and opened one of the bottles of
brandy. A small amount was poured into the
glasses, and lemonade was served for Jack
and his sister Emily.

"I say we drink the toast that poor Jem
never got the chance to drink," said Mr
Mutter.

Jack's mum peered closely at the dark liquid in her glass. "Will it still be safe to drink after all these years?"

"We'll soon find out," Mr Mutter replied. He raised his glass, which sparkled in the rays of sunshine pouring through the window. "To Jem, Edward Ford, and the gallant crew of the *Mayfly* – CHEERS!"

Fabulous Facts from ye Days of Smuggling!

1. This story is loosely based on a real life smuggler. Jack Rattenbury lived in a village called Beer in Devon (just along the coast from Lyme Regis) and did a lot of smuggling with his son William. (And one of his smuggling mates was called Abraham Mutter!)

2. Jack Rattenbury served for a time on board a Revenue cutter so he knew a lot about the enemy!

3. Not long after Jack Rattenbury's time, smuggling began to die out. The Revenue look-out posts and boats which had once caught smugglers began to rescue people in trouble at sea – and in the end became the modern Coast-guard service.

4. The Revenue men knew that smugglers sometimes threw their goods overboard, and used to go "creeping" for them. They rowed boats and dragged a sort of hook on the end of a rope through the water. If they were lucky, the hook would catch smugglers' sunken barrels.

5. Once they had carried their goods to shore, smugglers had lots of other clever hiding places. Barrels would be left inside caves, hollow trees, church towers - even empty tombs! Some houses, like the one in

this story, had double walls with a secret hiding place in between. Silk was once found inside some toy horses, and Jack Rattenbury even hid some inside a dead turkey which was meant for the dinner table!

6. Revenue cutters were built in a special way which made them the fastest small ships afloat. To make sure they could always catch any other boats, it was illegal for anyone else to build a boat in the same way. But of course in secret, the smugglers did!

7. Sometimes everyone in the village would be involved in smuggling in one way or another. It wasn't that the people were simply all criminals. Many were really very poor, and the taxes on some things like wine, tea and tobacco were impossibly high. Not only that, but even the price of things like bread had shot up because of the war. Often the only way some could make ends meet was to buy goods from France cheaply and sell them on at a price people could afford.

8. To be fair to the government at that time, however, there had just been a long and very expensive war. Today tax is taken out of the money people get paid for working, but that did not happen then. To provide money to run the country, the government put a tax on as many items as it could think of. Among other things, wigs

were taxed, hair powder, and even windows!
(Many people in bigger houses had some
windows bricked up so that they paid less
tax.)

Barrington Stoke would like to thank all its readers for commenting on the manuscript before publication and in particular:

Sara Byrne

Danny Figg

Sean Humber

Callum Maslen

Debbie Maslen

Michelle Morris

Katie Radford

Become a Consultant!

Would you like to give us feedback on our titles before they are published? Contact us at the email address below – we'd love to hear from you!

info@barringtonstoke.co.uk
www.barringtonstoke.co.uk

AUTHOR FACT FILE
MARTYN BEARDSLEY

What would you rather be – a smuggler or a Revenue man?

A Revenue man – most smugglers were very poor, and anyway I'd like to dress up in the uniform!

What's the most dangerous trip you've ever been on?

On the A1 to Cambridge stuck in a traffic jam and needing to go for a wee. I almost didn't make it!

What would you most like to find hidden in an old, rusty box?

A letter from the past like the one in the story. I've traced my own family tree and I love finding out more about people of long ago.

What goods would you like to smuggle, and why?

Tea – it was one of the main smuggled items. I drink gallons a day and can't write stories without it!

Where would you hide your goods from the Revenue men?

I think I'd build a fake toilet with horrible smells coming from it – they'd never look in there!

ILLUSTRATOR FACT FILE
DYLAN GIBSON

What would you rather be – a smuggler or a Revenue man?

Smuggler most definitely! When I was a kid I always wanted to play as Han Solo. He was a smuggler too!

What's the most dangerous trip you've ever been on?

On my mountain bike I go quite fast over trails and down hills! I've fallen off a few times and got bruised!

What would you most like to find hidden in an old, rusty box?

A map with the location of buried treasure or to a secret forgotten land!

What goods would you like to smuggle, and why?

Socks! Everybody needs socks!

Where would you hide your goods from the Revenue men?

I'm self-employed so I need to watch my tongue – they might be reading this!

Try another book in the "FYI" series!
Fiction with stacks of facts

Tracking/Environment
Tracking
by Gill Harvey

Maths
Counting on Leroy
by Steve Mills and Hilary Koll

The Romans
Assassin
by Tony Bradman

Surveillance
The Doomsday Watchers
by Steve Barlow and Steve Skidmore

All available from our website:
www.barringtonstoke.co.uk